Disney · PIXAR

INSIDE OUT 2

Disney Animation writing book

Disney · PIXAR

INSIDE OUT 2

Disney Animation writing book

글 신시아 리우 | 그림 앨런 뱃슨

더모던
Themodern

MEET *the* CHARACTERS

RILEY

Riley is now thirteen and navigating all the ups and downs of being a teenager! Excited to attend hockey camp with her best friends, Bree and Grace, Riley hopes they will get a spot on the Fire Hawks team in school next year! But things take a turn when Riley finds out that she and her besties won't be going to the same school. . . .

JOY

Always a **CHEERFUL OPTIMIST,** Joy will do whatever it takes to make sure that her girl, Riley, has an awesome life. Working with fellow Emotions Anger, Disgust, Fear, and Sadness, Joy has her tried-and-true plans to keep Riley happy and protect her Sense of Self. But all that changes the day some new Emotions show up!

ANGER

Though he can be pretty hot-headed and **EXPLOSIVE,** Anger is willing to risk anything and take any chances, all to get the very best for Riley.

DISGUST

Now that Riley is a teenager, Disgust's role is even more important. Disgust is in charge of knowing what's **COOL** and what isn't, and she isn't afraid to point out when something is totally **CRINGE**.

FEAR

Fear may be **OVERPROTECTIVE** of Riley, but that's only because he's always terrified. Fear's job is to keep Riley as **SAFE** as he can, so he's always on the lookout for danger.
But Fear can't possibly be prepared for what happens when the new Emotions arrive.

SADNESS

Besides being pretty sad, Sadness is not very confident in herself, but Joy knows that Sadness **HAS WHAT IT TAKES** to help make Riley's life amazing. Constantly concerned that she might do something to ruin everything, Sadness must learn to overcome her self-doubt when the new Emotions appear!

MEET *the* CHARACTERS

ANXIETY

Anxiety is **NERVOUS** and worried, to say the least. Always thinking ten steps ahead, Anxiety has sworn to be prepared for every possible pitfall in Riley's life, to make sure she fits in with her peers and never makes a mistake . . . no matter what Anxiety has to do to make it happen.

EMBARRASSMENT

Embarrassment is **BIG, AWKWARD,** very **SHY,** and clumsy, but he has a big heart. While he can't turn invisible, Embarrassment does the next best thing to make himself feel less noticed: he pulls the drawstring on his hoodie tight, closing it around his face. It kind of works. . . .

ENVY

SMALL but **MIGHTY**, Envy helps Riley figure out what she wants. Unfortunately, Envy wants a lot and doesn't always appreciate what Riley already has! When Envy sets her sights on Riley becoming a part of the varsity hockey team, she won't let Riley's best friends, Bree and Grace, get in the way.

ENNUI

Ennui prefers to stay put on her couch in Headquarters. She's too **BORED** to get up, so she drives the console by using an app on her phone. Ennui doesn't care about anything, which is valuable to teenage Riley, who's trying to appear **COOL** to her friends.

Thirteen-year-old Riley was the star hockey player for the Foghorns. They won the championship game! Riley's Emotions—Joy, Sadness, Anger, Fear, and Disgust—never stopped supporting their girl. They had helped her build a beautiful Sense of Self from her beliefs and memories. It said, "I'm a good person."

Thirteen-year-old Riley was the star hockey player for the Foghorns. They won the championship game!
Riley's **Emotions**–Joy, Sadness, **Anger**, **Fear**, and Disgust–never stopped **supporting** their girl. They had helped her build a beautiful Sense of Self from her **beliefs** and memories. It said, "I'm a good person."

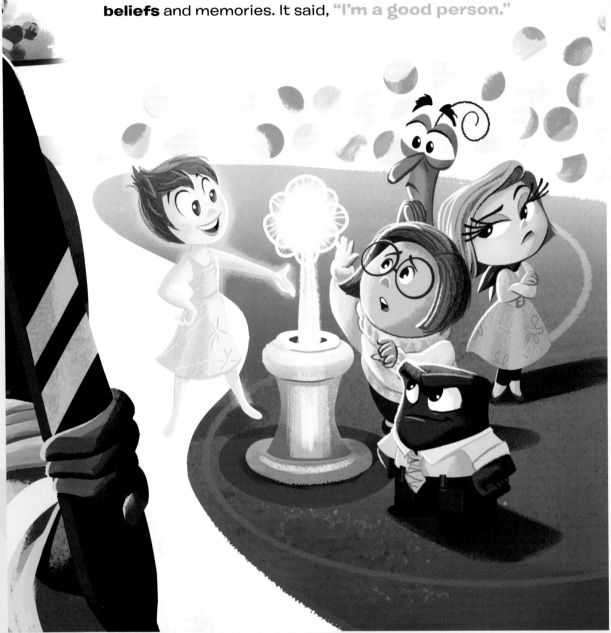

emotion : any strong feeling
support : the activity of providing for or maintaining by supplying with money or necessities
belief : any cognitive content held as true

Word	Definition

Riley was invited to a hockey camp. It was run by the coach from Riley's future high school team, the Fire Hawks. Riley remembered **past mistakes** she'd made and wondered if she'd be good enough for the team.

But Joy wasn't worried at all. Any bad memory that made Riley upset went straight to the **Back of the Mind**.

Joy and Sadness brought Riley's good memory of winning the game to the **Belief System**, where Riley's beliefs formed. The new belief that grew from the memory made Riley's **Sense of Self** glow even brighter.

Riley was **invited** to a hockey camp. It was run by the coach from Riley's future high school team, the Fire Hawks. Riley remembered past mistakes she'd made and wondered if she'd be good enough for the team.

But Joy wasn't **worried** at all. Any bad memory that made Riley upset went straight to the **Back of the Mind**.

invite : a colloquial expression for invitation

mistake : a wrong action attributable to bad judgment or ignorance or inattention

worry : something or someone that causes anxiety

Word	Definition

Joy and Sadness brought Riley's good memory of winning the **game** to the **Belief System**, where Riley's beliefs formed. The new belief that grew from the memory made Riley's **Sense of Self** glow even **brighter**.

game : a contest with rules to determine a winner

sense : a general conscious awareness

bright : emitting or reflecting light readily or in large amounts

Word	Definition

Later that night, an alarm went off in Headquarters. *Beep! Beeep!*
    Suddenly, **Mind Workers** appeared. They **tore apart** the console and made a few updates. After all, Riley was a teenager now. It was time for some **big changes**!

The Emotions tried out the new console, but every time they pushed a button, Riley **overreacted**. First, she **snapped** at her mother. Then she **cried** about snapping at her mother! Was the console broken? The Emotions were afraid to use it.

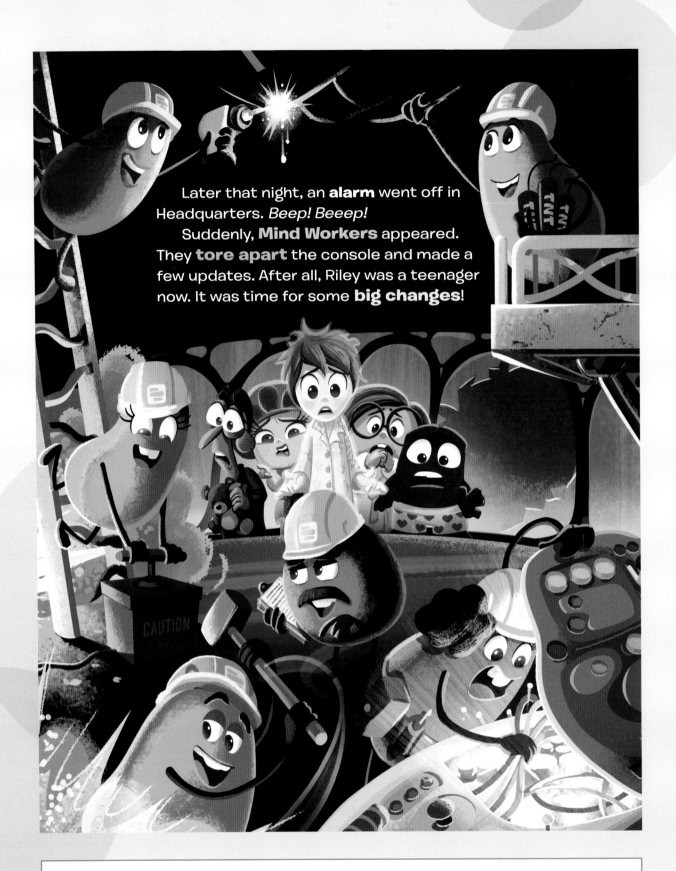

Later that night, an **alarm** went off in Headquarters. *Beep! Beeep!*
Suddenly, **Mind Workers** appeared. They **tore apart** the console and made a few updates. After all, Riley was a teenager now. It was time for some **big changes**!

alarm : fear resulting from the awareness of danger

tear : separate or cause to separate abruptly

change : the action of changing something

Word	Definition

The Emotions tried out the new console, but every time
they pushed a button, Riley **overreacted**. First, she **snapped**
at her mother. Then she **cried** about snapping at her mother!
Was the console broken? The Emotions were afraid to use it.

overreact : show an exaggerated response to something

snap : to break quickly with a short, sharp sound

cry : a fit of weeping

Word	Definition

Soon Riley was off to hockey camp with her friends Bree and Grace. But they had **bad news**: they'd been assigned to a different high school. Oh, no! What would Riley do without them next year?

Then Riley bumped into **Valentina Ortiz**, the Fire Hawks' captain. *Gulp!* Val was her hockey hero.

Back at Headquarters, Joy got her own surprise when four new Emotions arrived. **Anxiety** couldn't wait to help Riley. **Envy** wished she was as tall as everyone else. **Embarrassment** was sweet but not much of a talker. And **Ennui**? She was bored with everything except her phone.

Soon Riley was off to hockey camp with her friends Bree and Grace. But they had **bad news**: they'd been assigned to a different high school. Oh, no! What would Riley do without them next year?

Then Riley **bumped** into **Valentina Ortiz**, the Fire Hawks' captain. *Gulp!* Val was her hockey **hero**.

news : information about recent and important events

bump : a lump on the body caused by a blow

hero : a man distinguished by exceptional courage and nobility and strength

Word	Definition

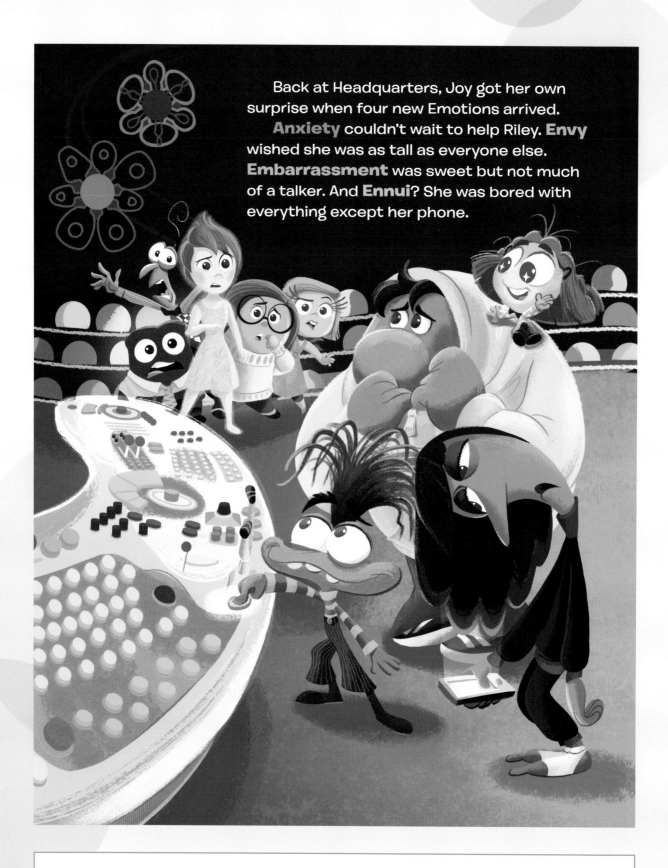

Back at Headquarters, Joy got her own surprise when four new Emotions arrived. **Anxiety** couldn't wait to help Riley. **Envy** wished she was as tall as everyone else. **Embarrassment** was sweet but not much of a talker. And **Ennui**? She was bored with everything except her phone.

anxiety : fear or nervousness about what might happen

envy : the feeling of wanting to have what someone else has

embarrassment : the state of feeling foolish in front of others

Word	Definition

Anxiety was determined to get Riley onto the Fire Hawks team so she would have friends in high school.

Joy thought Riley should **just have fun**. She inspired Riley to take silly selfies with Bree and Grace.

But the coach wanted them to focus. **She took away everyone's phones!** Riley was so embarrassed.

Anxiety was certain that Riley wouldn't make the team if she didn't change. She needed a newer and better Sense of Self to become a newer and better Riley. Anxiety **yanked the Sense of Self from its pedestal** and launched it to the Back of the Mind!

Anxiety was **determined** to get Riley onto the Fire Hawks team so she would have friends in high school. Joy thought Riley should just have fun. She **inspired** Riley to take silly selfies with Bree and Grace.

But the coach wanted them to **focus. She took away everyone's phones!** Riley was so **embarrassed**.

determine : decide upon or fix definitely

inspire : fill with revolutionary ideas

focus : the concentration of attention or energy on something

Word	Definition

Anxiety was certain that Riley wouldn't make the team if she didn't change. She needed a newer and better Sense of Self to become a newer and better Riley. Anxiety **yanked the Sense of Self from its pedestal** and launched it to the Back of the Mind!

yank : pull, or move with a sudden movement

pedestal : a support or foundation

Word	Definition

When Joy and the other Emotions protested, Anxiety sent them to the vault, where Riley's secrets were kept. Trapped inside, they met **Bloofy** and **Pouchy**, characters from a preschool TV show that Riley secretly still liked. **Lance Slashblade** was a video game hero that she had a crush on. And Riley's **Deep Dark Secret** was, well . . . you don't want to know.

Pouchy offered some items to help them escape.
Anger chose the **exploding dynamite**!

When Joy and the other Emotions **protested**, Anxiety sent them to the **vault**, where Riley's **secrets** were kept. Trapped inside, they met **Bloofy** and **Pouchy**, characters from a preschool TV show that Riley secretly still liked. **Lance Slashblade** was a video game hero that she had a crush on. And Riley's **Deep Dark Secret** was, well . . . you don't want to know.

Pouchy offered some items to help them escape.
Anger chose the **exploding dynamite**!

protest : to show or express strong disagreement with or disapproval of something

vault : a burial chamber

secret : not open or public

Word	Definition

The Emotions had to hurry to the Back of the Mind to find Riley's old Sense of Self. But they needed some help from Headquarters. It was up to Sadness to sneak in through the Recall Tube!

The rest of the Emotions followed the Stream of Consciousness, which carried objects that Riley was thinking about. It would lead them to the Back of the Mind.

The Emotions had to hurry to the Back of the Mind to find Riley's old Sense of Self. But they needed some help from Headquarters. It was up to Sadness to **sneak in through the Recall Tube**!

The rest of the Emotions followed the **Stream** of **Consciousness**, which carried objects that Riley was thinking about. It would lead them to the Back of the Mind.

sneak : marked by quiet and caution and secrecy
stream : a natural body of running water flowing on or under the earth
consciousness : an alert cognitive state in which you are aware of yourself and your situation

Word	Definition

Along their journey, the Emotions discovered that Anxiety was ordering Mind Workers to imagine **everything that could go wrong** for Riley. Anxiety believed this would help prepare her for the final game at camp. But it made Riley super stressed!

So Joy started imagining things going right for Riley. One by one, the Mind Workers **joined her**! But then the Mind Police showed up! The Emotions escaped by soaring away on a giant balloon.

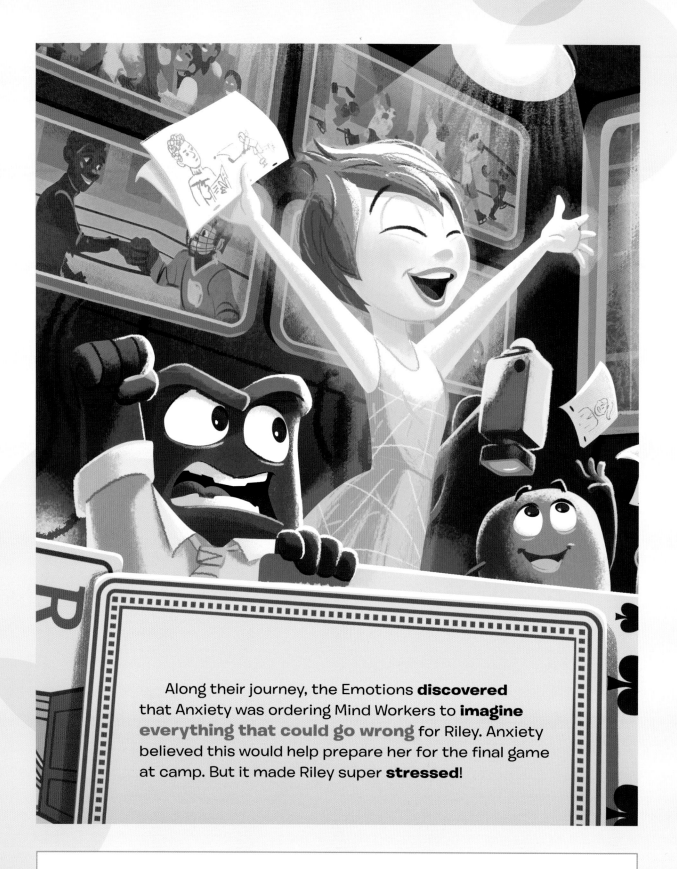

Along their journey, the Emotions **discovered** that Anxiety was ordering Mind Workers to **imagine everything that could go wrong** for Riley. Anxiety believed this would help prepare her for the final game at camp. But it made Riley super **stressed**!

discover : to see, find, or become aware of (something) for the first time

imagine : form a mental image of something that is not present or that is not the case

stress : a state of mental tension and worry caused by problems in your life, work, etc.

Word	Definition

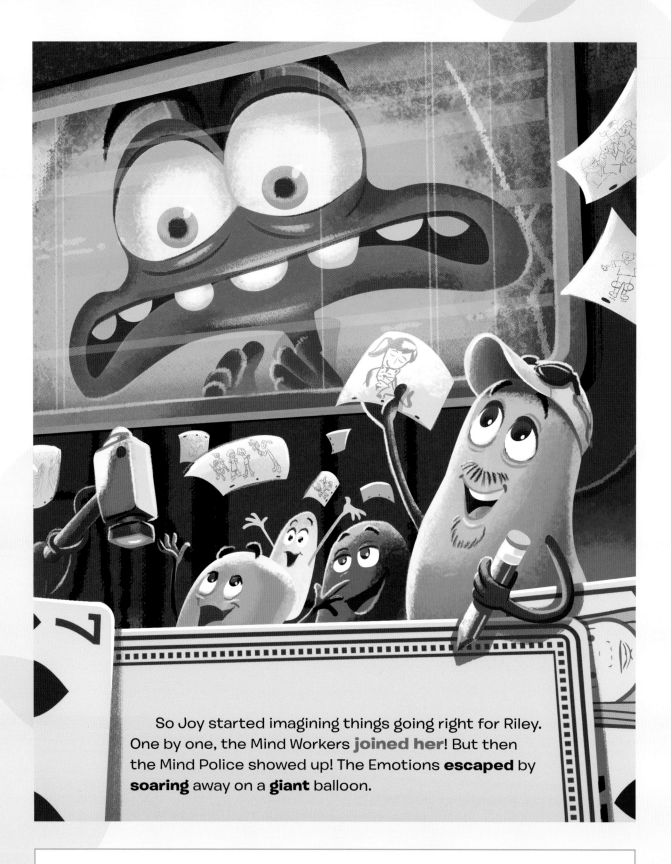

So Joy started imagining things going right for Riley. One by one, the Mind Workers **joined her**! But then the Mind Police showed up! The Emotions **escaped** by **soaring** away on a **giant** balloon.

escape : to get away from a dangerous place or situation

soar : to rise quickly upward to a great height

giant : very large, much larger or more powerful than normal

Word	Definition

Anxiety needed a new plan—and ideas—to prepare Riley
for the game. She started a **brainstorm**!

Ideas rained from the sky, pummeling the Emotions
and their balloon. It was going to pop! Suddenly, **a big
idea swooped by**. The Emotions leapt onto the idea and
soared out of the storm!

Now Riley was ready for the game. She tried to look and act like a Fire Hawk. Grace and Bree **hardly knew their best friend anymore**.

Meanwhile, the Emotions finally reached the Back of the Mind. They discovered a **massive mountain** of all the bad memories Joy had thrown away. Riley's old Sense of Self was at the top!

Anxiety needed a new **plan**—and ideas—to prepare Riley for the game. She started a **brainstorm**!

Ideas rained from the sky, pummeling the Emotions and their balloon. It was going to pop! Suddenly, a big idea swooped by. The Emotions leapt onto the idea and soared out of the storm!

plan : a set of actions that have been thought of as a way to do or achieve something

brainstorm : an idea that someone thinks of suddenly

swoop : to fly down through the air suddenly

Word	Definition

Now Riley was ready for the game. She tried to look and act like a Fire Hawk. Grace and Bree **hardly knew their best friend anymore**.

Meanwhile, the Emotions finally reached the Back of the Mind. They discovered a **massive mountain** of all the bad memories Joy had **thrown away**. RIley's old Sense of Self was at the top!

---

massive : very large and heavy

thrown away : to put (something that is no longer useful or wanted) in a trash can, garbage can, rubbish bin, etc.

Word	Definition

Back in Headquarters, Sadness got caught before she could help her friends. But it was already too late. Anxiety had created a new Sense of Self! It now said, **"I'm not good enough."**

Anxiety pushed Riley even harder. But during the big game, Riley doubted herself. **The pressure was too much**—for her and for Anxiety.

Joy and the Emotions found Riley's old Sense of Self, but without Sadness's help, they had to figure out a new way to return to Headquarters. They released the memories, **sending them tumbling** toward the Belief System. The four friends went along for the ride!

Back in Headquarters, Sadness got caught before she could help her friends. But it was already too late. Anxiety had **created** a new Sense of Self! It now said, "I'm not good enough."

Anxiety **pushed** Riley even harder. But during the big game, Riley doubted herself. **The pressure was too much**—for her and for Anxiety.

create : make or cause to be or to become

push : the act of applying force in order to move something away

pressure : to use pressure to force or try to force (someone) to do something

Word	Definition

Joy and the Emotions found Riley's old Sense of Self, but without Sadness's help, they had to **figure out** a new way to return to Headquarters. They released the memories, **sending them tumbling** toward the **Belief** System. The four friends went along for the ride!

figure out : to understand or find (something, such as a reason or a solution) by thinking

tumble : to fall down suddenly and quickly

belief : a feeling of being sure that someone or something exists or that something is true

Word	Definition

As the bad memories poured into the Belief System, new beliefs sprouted, creating a glow that was brighter than ever before! The beliefs began to form **Riley's true Sense of Self**—one that included the good, the bad, and everything in between.

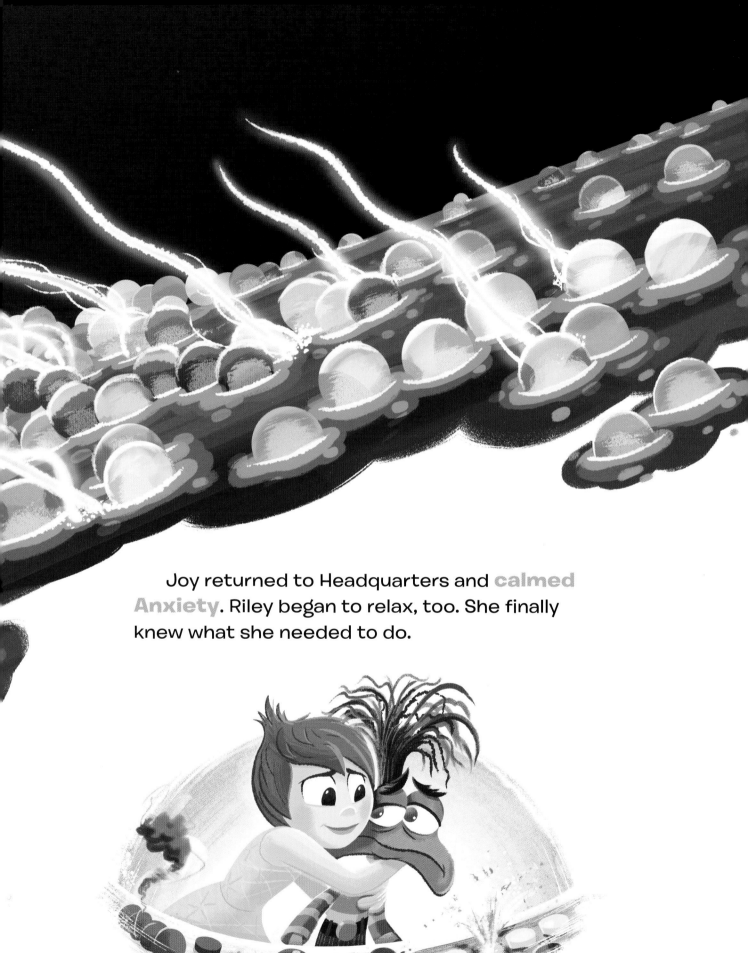

Joy returned to Headquarters and calmed
Anxiety. Riley began to relax, too. She finally
knew what she needed to do.

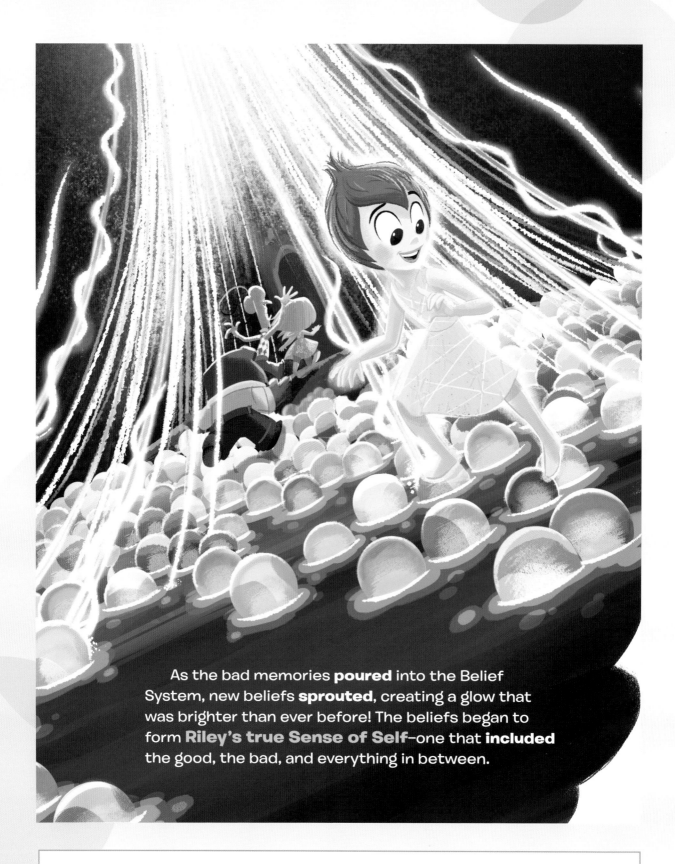

As the bad memories **poured** into the Belief System, new beliefs **sprouted**, creating a glow that was brighter than ever before! The beliefs began to form **Riley's true Sense of Self**—one that **included** the good, the bad, and everything in between.

pour : to cause (something) to flow in a steady stream from or into a container or place

sprout : any new growth of a plant such as a new branch or a bud

include : have as a part, be made up out of

Word	Definition

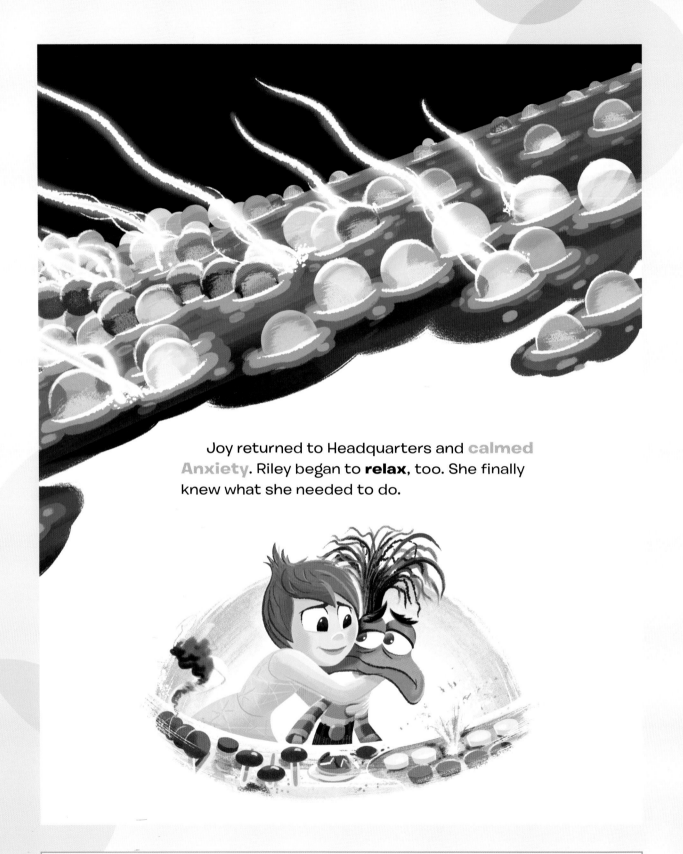

Joy returned to Headquarters and calmed Anxiety. Riley began to **relax**, too. She finally knew what she needed to do.

calm : to become or to cause (someone) to become less upset, emotional, excited, etc.

relax : become less tense, rest, or take one's ease

Word	Definition

Riley apologized to her friends. She'd been feeling uncertain about herself and the future. But her friends–both old and new–would be there to support her. **Riley wasn't alone.**

Even though Riley and her Sense of Self were still changing, the Emotions knew one thing: they would always love their girl.

Riley **apologized** to her friends. She'd been feeling uncertain about herself and the future. But her friends–both old and new–would be there to **support** her. Riley wasn't alone.

Even though Riley and her Sense of Self were still changing, the Emotions knew one thing: they would always love their girl.

apologize : express regret for doing or saying something wrong, to give or make an apology

support : the act of helping someone by giving love, encouragement, etc.

Word	Definition

글 신시아 리우 | 그림 앨런 뱃슨

1판 1쇄 펴낸 날 | 2024년 12월 25일

펴낸이   장영재
펴낸곳   (주)미르북컴퍼니
자회사   더모던
전 화   02)3141-4421
팩 스   0505-333-4428
등 록   2012년 3월 16일(제313-2012-81호)
주 소   서울시 마포구 성미산로32길 12, 2층 (우 03983)
e-mail   sanhonjinju@naver.com
카 페   cafe.naver.com/mirbookcompany
인스타그램 www.instagram.com/mirbooks

KC인증정보 품명 아동 도서 **사용연령** 4~7세 **제조년월일** 2024년 12월 25일 **제조국** 대한민국 **연락처**
02)3141-4421 서울시 마포구 성미산로32길 12, 2층 **주의사항** 종이에 베이거나 긁히지 않도록 조심하세요.
책 모서리가 날카로우니 던지거나 떨어뜨리지 마세요.